Why can't I fly?

Written by Anna Cowper

Illustrated by Alice Negri

Collins

What's in this book?

Listen and say 🎧①

airship

helicopter

bird

Download the audio at www.collins.co.uk/839838

sky

hot air balloon

cloud

plane

Grandad says, "Look at the beautiful birds! Look at them flying high in the sky! They are so happy."

Birds are small and light, but
people are big and heavy.

Lots of people want to fly.
Some people made machines.

Some people made wings. They climbed to high places ... and jumped!

But in the end, when people try to fly, we always CRASH!

People can fly in balloons! This is a hot air balloon. The gas inside the balloon makes the balloon go up and up.

Up in the sky, it's very quiet.
Balloons don't make any noise when
they fly.

Look! The children can see their house and
their school. The people are so small.

Inside the cloud it is cold and wet, and you can't see much.

We're coming out of the cloud now.
We can see the sun again. That's better!

Up in the sky, it's always cold. It's colder than on the ground.

Birds have feathers to keep them warm. We put on warm clothes.

feathers

Another way people can fly is in an airship.

Airships are very big balloons.

They can carry a lot of people.

There are places for people to sit, eat and sleep.

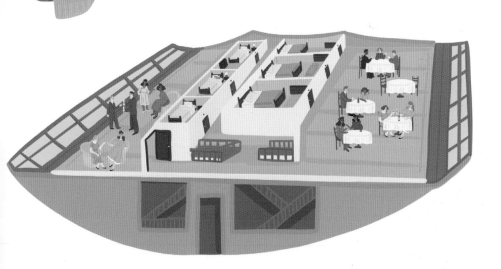

But we don't use airships now.
They are slow.

We use planes to fly. Planes go very fast.

They are much faster than birds or hot air
balloons. They are much noisier, too.

Planes are very big!
They are heavy, too.

With all those people inside
they are VERY heavy.

How do they fly?

Planes fly because they have engines and wings.

The engines make the plane go very fast.

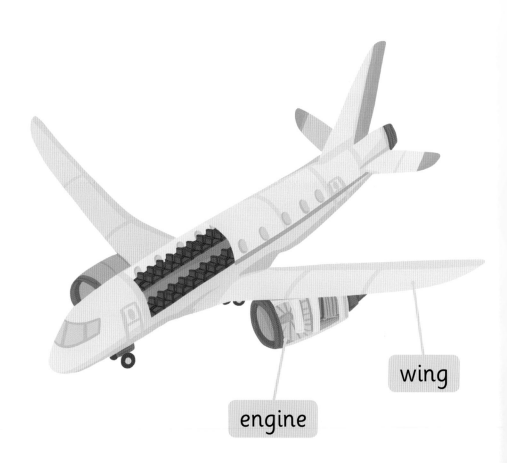

engine

wing

The engines make the plane go faster and faster.

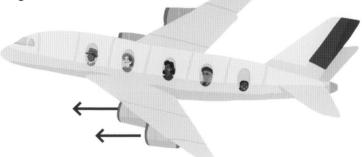

The air moves faster over and slower under the wings.

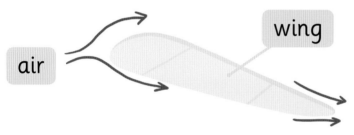

The air under the wings pushes the plane up into the sky.

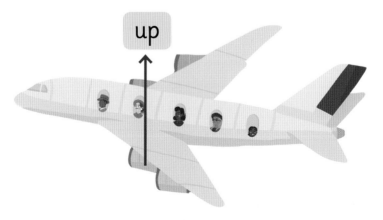

Helicopters don't have wings.

They have blades. Blades go round and round very fast.

They make lots of noise and lots of wind. The wind takes the helicopter up into the sky.

blades

Helicopters can go forwards, backwards and turn around.

Birds and planes can't go backwards!

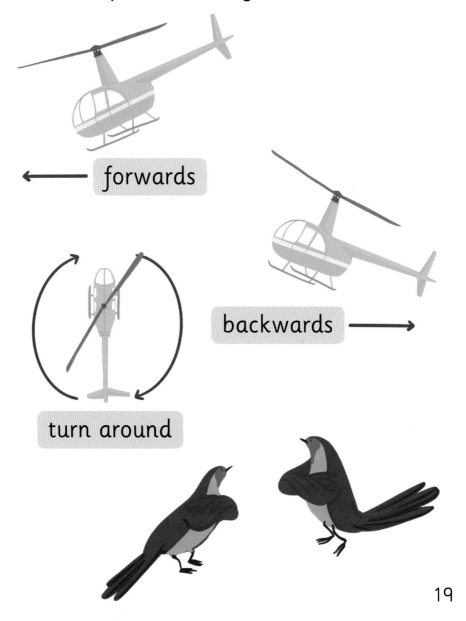

forwards

backwards

turn around

We use helicopters to help people.
A car can't drive up a mountain,
but a helicopter can fly there.

So, you see, people can fly. They can fly in balloons, airships, planes and helicopters.

Maybe, one day, you can learn to fly, too.

Picture dictionary

Listen and repeat

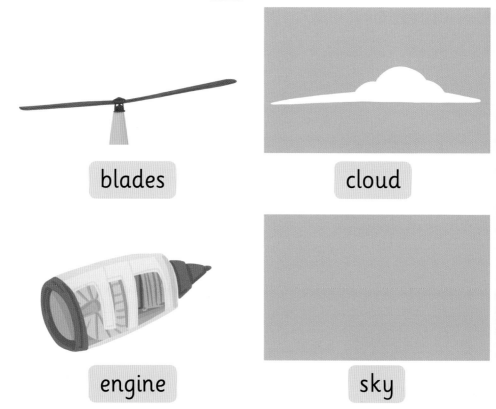

blades

cloud

engine

sky

wing

1 Look and match

plane   hot air balloon

helicopter   airship

2 Listen and say

Collins

Published by Collins
An imprint of HarperCollins*Publishers*
Westerhill Road
Bishopbriggs
Glasgow
G64 2QT

HarperCollins*Publishers*
1st Floor, Watermarque Building
Ringsend Road
Dublin 4
Ireland

William Collins' dream of knowledge for all began with the publication of his first book in 1819.

A self-educated mill worker, he not only enriched millions of lives, but also founded a flourishing publishing house. Today, staying true to this spirit, Collins books are packed with inspiration, innovation and practical expertise. They place you at the centre of a world of possibility and give you exactly what you need to explore it.

© HarperCollins*Publishers* Limited 2020

10 9 8 7 6 5 4 3 2

ISBN 978-0-00-839838-5

Collins® and COBUILD® are registered trademarks of HarperCollins*Publishers* Limited

www.collins.co.uk/elt

British Library Cataloguing in Publication Data

A catalogue record for this publication is available from the British Library.

Author: Anna Cowper
Illustrator: Alice Negri (Beehive)
Series editor: Rebecca Adlard
Publishing manager: Lisa Todd
Product managers: Jennifer Hall and Caroline Green
In-house editor: Alma Puts Keren
Project manager: Emily Hooton
Editor: Frances Amrani
Proofreaders: Natalie Murray and Michael Lamb
Cover designer: Kevin Robbins
Typesetter: 2Hoots Publishing Services Ltd
Audio produced by id audio, London
Reading guide author: Emma Wilkinson
Production controller: Rachel Weaver
Printed and bound by: GPS Group, Slovenia

Download the audio for this book and a reading guide for parents and teachers at www.collins.co.uk/839838